Sometimey friend

Other books by Pansie Hart Flood

Sylvia & Miz Lula Maye
Secret Holes

Sometimey friend

Pansie Hart Flood

illustrated by
Felicia Marshall

🌿 Carolrhoda Books, Inc./Minneapolis

Carolrhoda Books, Inc.
A division of Lerner Publishing Group
241 First Avenue North
Minneapolis, MN 55401 U.S.A.

Website address: www.lernerbooks.com

Library of Congress Cataloging-in-Publication Data

Flood, Pansie Hart.
    Sometimey friend / by Pansie Hart Flood ; illustrated by Felicia Marshall.
       p.   cm.
    Sequel to: Sylvia and Miz Lula Maye.
    Summary: When her mother goes to Florida in 1978, ten-year-old Sylvia
stays behind in South Carolina, but when she fails to make new friends at
school, she realizes that her newly discovered great-grandmother and best
friend, Miz Lula Maye, might be the problem.
    ISBN-13: 978–1–57505–866–5 (lib. bdg. : alk. paper)
    ISBN-10: 1–57505–866–9 (lib. bdg. : alk. paper)
    [1. Family life—South Carolina—Fiction. 2. Great-grandmothers—
Fiction. 3. Schools—Fiction. 4. Old age—Fiction. 5. African
Americans—Fiction. 6. South Carolina—Fiction.] I. Marshall, Felicia, ill.
II. Title.
PZ7.F66185So 2005
[Fic]—dc22   2004027724

Manufactured in the United States of America
1 2 3 4 5 6 – BP – 10 09 08 07 06 05

In memory of my beloved grandmother, whose existence
inspired me to create the character Miz Lula Maye

Pearlie Mae Reaves Wallace
1892–2000

Also, for Merrill, Jasmine, and Joey for unconditional love,
support, patience, and belief in my writing

Contents

ONE

Thinkin'

Way Out Yonder

Me, Miz Lula Maye, and Cousin Jack Jr. were sitting in a steamy, hot, two-hundred-degrees, beat-up old car withs no air conditioner. The windows were rolled down as far as they could go.

"Sylvia, what's takin' your momma so long?" asked Miz Lula Maye. "She's gonna miss the train if we don't hurry."

I shook my head, meaning I don't know. Momma fixin' ready to leave me for the first time was a bit scary. I mean, I felt safe stayin' withs Miz Lula Maye. She's my great-grandma 'n all, and I love being with her. Me and Momma just hadn't ever been apart. For now, though, I was doin' a good job at keepin' my mind occupied thinkin' 'bout stuff way out yonder. Like for instance, clothes.

It felt extra super hot today 'cause we were all dressed up for church. To me, it seems like church clothes is the hottest and most uncomfortable clothes in the whole wide world.

If you going to church and you're a girl or lady, then you gots to wear a dress. If you wearin' a dress, you gots to wear a slip and stockings or panty hose or tights or socks, depending on the shoes you're wearing, which depends on your age.

Miz Lula Maye was born way back in 1878. It's 1978, so that means she's one hundred years old. She wears a slip no matter how hot it gets. As for stockings, Miz Lula Maye says, "If it's too hot, I takes 'em off." One thing she won't take off is her hat. Miz Lula Maye loves her hats 'bout as much as she loves her cats.

As for me, thank God I'm still young enough to wear dressy bobby socks, which means my legs were bare. I'm almost eleven. So when I wears a dress to church in the hot summer, my skinny little legs gets fresh air. Even though it's hot, air is air.

Momma finally came out of our house with her hands full of stuff she was taking with her. "Well, it's about time!" Jack Jr. said, taking her bags and putting them in the trunk.

Momma got in the backseat next to me. She was wearin' my favorite dress. This dusty rose-colored dress has tiny little burgundy roses spread all over it. The material is so thin, it looks like a big scarf that a movie star might wear on her head while riding in a car with no roof. Straight down the dress from top to bottom is a single row of beautiful buttons that looks like pearls. Just like the kind you'd make a pearl necklace with.

Momma looked so pretty all dressed up like she was goin' to church. But she wasn't goin' to church. Jack Jr. was driving her to the train station uptown in Dillon. I hadn't ever been to the train station before. Momma and me came into Wakeview, South Carolina, at the beginning of summer on a bus from Florida. That's when my whole life changed like a butterfly.

The truth about me and Momma is that Momma is really my aunt. My real momma died when I was just a baby. Momma raised me the best she could, workin' in the fields in places like Alabama and Florida. She didn't have no help because all of the rest of her family was gone. When Momma got tired of doin' everything on her own, we came up to Wakeview, 'cause that's where my daddy was from. I guess she thought I might have family here that could help out.

Here's the thing, though. I didn't know about any of this when we came here. When it comes to the big F, meaning Family, Momma had a lot of secrets. For a long time, I thought Momma was my momma and my daddy was dead. I also thought that the lady who lived at the end of my road, Miz Lula Maye, was just my bestest friend in the whole world. And I thought silly-actin' Jack Jr. was just her nephew who took care of her.

Well, the truth came out when my daddy, Mr. Jonathan Maye, showed up to visit Miz Lula Maye 'cause she is his grandma. Now I have a daddy who is alive, I have a crazy cousin, and I have a best friend who is also my great-grandma. And Momma is still Momma, even though she's my aunt.

I like havin' family. That was a part of me that

had been missin' in my life. Now it was Momma's turn. She was on her way to a weird-sounding place in Florida called Okaloosa to see if she could find some of her family.

Nobody in the car talked on the way to the train station. Couldn't hear anything, nohow. If anybody did talk with all the windows rolled down, we'd have to yell over the wind just to be heard.

All that silence gave my brain permission to start frettin'. What if something happens and it's something that only Momma can takes care of? I worried. Shucks, by the time she'd get the word and travel all the way back to Wakeview—heck, I'd be dead and gone to my grave by then.

I knew I was gonna have hard homework once I started back to school. What if I need help? I thought. Miz Lula Maye is smart, but schools are teachin' a bunch of new stuff these days. Miz Lula Maye or Jack Jr. don't know nothing about the new stuff. Can't call all the way to Florida just to ask some stupid homework questions about math or social studies. And what if I have to take French? I didn't realize it until then, but

I was really gonna need my momma.

"Lord, Lord, help me please," I whispered.

When we got to the train station, Momma's train was just pulling up. It was metal, silver-looking with red, white, and blue stripes, just like an American flag.

"Wow!" I said. "Is that your train, Momma?"

"I think it might be," said Momma.

I was totally puzzled. "What happened to the real-looking trains like the ones on TV? This train almost looks like something from out of space."

Jack Jr. laughed at me as he helped Momma get her bags out of the car. Me and Miz Lula Maye headed to the station. I wanted to touch the train, but I was too scared. Didn't know for sure, but I thought it might burn my fingers. It looked really fast. And it was gonna take my momma from me.

Momma bought her ticket, and then it was time for her to go. She came over and brushed my back as if I had dandruff or something on my dress. Then she took my hand and rubbed the inside of my palm. It felt nice, like a massage. She traced all the lines on my palm.

"Sylvia, I expects you to mind Miz Lula Maye. No back talk, keep your room clean, and help Miz Lula Maye with housekeepin'."

"Yes, ma'am," I said. I felt like cryin', but cryin' wouldn't change the plan. So I didn't cry.

"I love you, Sylvia, and Lord knows, I'm gonna miss my baby," Momma said. "Be a good girl. I'll be back before too long, okay?"

Momma hugged Miz Lula Maye and Jack Jr. Then she kissed me on my cheek, squeezed me real tight, and got on the fancy silver American train. The doors on the train closed automatically, just like elevators. Momma waved goodbye in her window as the train pulled off. Gradually, minute by minute, it picked up speed. Then it disappeared like through thin air. The back of the train was there one second and gone the next.

"It's alright to cry," Miz Lula Maye whispered. She put her arm around me and squeezed my shoulder. It was a hot, steamy day outside. But on the inside, my bones felt cold, like I was standin' in snow wearin' these same summer clothes.

We drove back to Wakeview and went on to

church. Pastor Stevens had already started preaching, so we had to sit near the back. Of course, Miz Lula Maye was not happy about that. She usually sits on the first pew.

After the service, we all went into the fellowship hall to have our end-of-summer dinner. I thought Miz Lula Maye's one-hundredth birthday party had a lot of food. Not so. There was enough food at this dinner to feed millions. And folks were packed up in the fellowship hall like it was gonna be their last supper.

I wasn't hungry. It was too doggone hot in there to be eating, anyways. I threw my plate full of food in the trash and went outside to sit under a huge, shady magnolia tree. That's where I was, mindin' my own business, when Taylor Jones came out of the church. No way, I thought. Not TJ and me outside by ourselves.

I eased up slowly from the ground where I was sitting. Very slowly and carefully, I inched around to the back side of the tree. Surely, I was well hidden 'cause this magnolia tree was huge. Standing as quietly as I could, I hoped that I'd spotted Taylor Jones before he'd spotted me. And most definitely, I hoped Taylor Jones absolutely did not see me hide behind the magnolia tree like some scary cat.

From the first Sunday I went to church with Miz Lula Maye, this big-headed, not quite fat, but chunky or big-boned boy called Taylor Jones started to biting at my nerves. I guess it's safe to call a boy big boned. Usually people refers to females as being big boned. Anyways, that's what Taylor Jones is to me, the way I sees it. He would do things like smiles at me and don't say nothing. In exchange for his smiling at me, I'd roll my eyes at him and say nothing. Then with his stupid self, he'd smile back after me. I'd say to myself, "Is he wacko or what?"

Maybe that's why he comes to church, I thought. He's crazy and comes to church to see if God can make him uncrazy. That's it! Taylor Jones comes to Miz Lula Maye's church to be healed, healed by the Holy Ghost. I wonder how long has he been coming to church. Wonder how long will it take for him to be healed from being both stupid and crazy.

Things had gotten quiet under the magnolia

tree. I figured Taylor Jones musta gone back into the fellowship hall. I peeped over my shoulder around the tree. The coast was definitely clear. I stepped away from the tree, and wouldn't you know it, there was Taylor Jones with his back up against the other side of the tree!

"Taylor Jones!" I hollered. "Boy, you just scared the skin off of me! What's wrong with you, sneakin' up under trees, scarin' folks?"

Taylor Jones didn't open his mouth and say a word. He just looked at me and smiled. Then he walked away.

"Crazy—that's what he is—C-R-A-Z-Y," I said to myself. But I have to admit, I had kinda stopped missing Momma for a little while.

Chapter  TWO

Myrtle

Beach

I fell asleep Sunday night waiting for Momma to call. Guess she never got around to it. The next morning when I woke up, Miz Lula Maye came and sat on the edge of my bed.

"How did this old bed sleep last night? You didn't feel any springs pokin' you in the back, did ya?" she asked.

I shook my head. "Miz Lula Maye, you heard from my momma yet?"

"Nah. Surely she traveled all day. Probably got there late in the evenin'. Soon as she gets a chance, I'm sure she'll give us a ring." Miz Lula Maye looked at my face. "Don't go to thinkin' she's done and forgotten about you. Much as your momma loves you, ain't no way she's gonna forget to call."

I leaned over and put my head on Miz Lula Maye's shoulder. "Well, I reckon so. Just thought I would've heard from her by now."

Miz Lula Maye put her arms around me and squeezed. "Let's have a quick breakfast. I've got something mighty special planned for today."

I looked up at Miz Lula Maye. Maybe today wouldn't be so bad. "I love surprises!" I said. "What is it?"

"Jack Jr. will be coming over here directly to take us to Myrtle Beach," she answered. "We're gonna take you shoppin' for school. Ain't that dandy?" Miz Lula Maye gave me one more squeeze and stood up.

I didn't say anything 'cause I didn't want to ruin Miz Lula Maye's surprise. But all I was thinking about was hearing my momma's voice. If we left the house to go school shopping in Myrtle Beach, I might miss the phone call.

I got up and followed Miz Lula Maye to the kitchen. I sat down at the table and started playin' with the salt-'n-pepper shakers. Miz Lula Maye turned around and leaned up against the sink, watching me. Finally she said, "Sylvia, what's on your mind, baby?"

"What if Momma calls while we're gone?" I asked.

"So you want to sit here all day waiting on the phone to ring?"

"No," I said and put my head down on the table. Now I was really startin' to feel sorry for myself. "I ain't got no money for shoppin', anyway. Momma didn't leave me with a red cent."

"Child, you's pitiful," said Miz Lula Maye. "You ought to know better by now that I'm here for you. If I says we's goin' shoppin', then that means I'm payin'. Now I'm here to tell ya, Sylvia, that I'm not sittin' 'round here all day waiting for a phone to ring. Lord knows I loves you, but you can sit here by yourself."

Miz Lula Maye got me good. She knew I wasn't 'bout to stay home all day by myself. She started to fry up some eggs, and I got up to help her.

I'm beginning to figure out that Jack Jr. has some kind of food-detecting radar. He always comes in at just the right time—when it's time to eat. Does he ever come early to help cook? Nope! He's got it made in the shade. And does Miz Lula Maye ask him to help clean up the kitchen? Nope again!

"Howdy! Looks like I'm just in time!" Jack Jr. said as he entered the kitchen.

I turned around and almost dropped a basket full of toasted light bread. Why? 'Cause when I saw what Jack Jr. was wearin', I 'bout had a serious laughing attack. He was dressed like some mixed-up, no-matching cowboy man from the Wild West. His pants were a lot too tight and were almost high waters. Plus he was wearing light brown fuzzy-looking boots, with pointed toes 'n all. UGLY! To top everything off, I could hear the wide baby blue suede belt hanging low on his waist and the white V-neck T-shirt yelling, "Save me! I don't match! Save me!"

"This here vest and pants is the real deal, Cousin Sylvia," Jack Jr. said in a serious and convincing voice. "It's all genuine cowhide leather."

"He's sharp ain't he, Sylvia?" Miz Lula Maye chuckled. "What you all dressed up for?"

"We going to Myrtle Beach, ain't we?" Jack Jr. asked.

"Well, that's up to Sylvia," Miz Lula Maye answered looking at me.

I was dressed and ready in a flash.

It took us about forty-five minutes to get to Myrtle Beach. Miz Lula Maye and Jack Jr. let me listen to my kind of music on the radio. I stretched out in the backseat and pretended to be the lead singer in every song.

I was singing with the Commodores when I spotted the ocean. "Myrtle Beach is really a beach!" I said.

"What did you think it would be?" said Jack Jr. smirking. I ignored him and breathed in as deep as I could. I could smell the ocean. Once you know that smell, you never forget.

"That's the Atlantic Ocean," said Miz Lula Maye. "It's the same ocean you grew up around in Florida."

We drove down the main strip of Myrtle Beach. It was like a gigantic carnival. The sidewalks were so jam-packed that most people walked in the street.

"Is it always this crowded?" I asked.

Miz Lula Maye told me it was especially packed with people because this day was a holiday called Labor Day. She said it was the day people take off from their job to celebrate having a job, which I thought was funny.

"It's also the official last day of summertime, so everyone comes out to play," said Jack Jr.

People sho' was doin' some celebrating. There was all sorts of stuff to buy, like T-shirts and sand castle buckets and big straw hats. People was ridin' bumper cars and go-carts, and playin' games to win prizes. I looked up and saw a big Ferris wheel goin' 'round.

I stuck my head out the car window as far as I could without falling out. Now I couldn't smell the ocean. Instead, I smelled corn dogs, french fries, and fried chicken. Big signs with flashing lights said they had ice cream, foot-long hot dogs, lemonade, cotton candy, candied apples, popcorn, roasted peanuts, burgers, sausage dogs, and corn on the cob, too. I saw so much, closing my eyes made me feel dizzy.

It took Jack Jr. a long time to find a parking

space. "I hope this ain't too far for you to walk," he said to Miz Lula Maye when we got out of the car.

Miz Lula Maye stopped in the middle of the crowded sidewalk and put her hands on her hips. She looked Jack Jr. straight in his eyes and said, "I ain't that old, Jack. Do I look cripple? Do I need a cane to get around? I been walkin' all my life. I walked eight miles every day to school—in the rain, in the hot sun, in the cold, and even in the snow. I can probably outwalk you!"

Miz Lula Maye and Jack Jr. loves to fuss with each other. It's so funny listening to those two. They both really cracks me up. I'm smart, too. I stay out of it when they starts up at each other. I just listen and laugh.

First we walked into a store that only sold shoes. Don't know when I've been to a real shoe store trying on brand-new shoes. In Florida, me and Momma always shopped at secondhand stores. Momma says those kind of stores is where you really get your money's worth.

Miz Lula Maye must be rich. And this musta been my lucky day. I found a brand-new pair of tan and navy blue saddle oxfords in just the right

size. That's 'cause the saleslady measured my foot first. Miz Lula Maye let me wear my new shoes out of the store. We put my raggedy old sandals in the new shoe box.

Next we went to a clothes store. I wanted to look at pants, but Miz Lula Maye wanted me to look at boring dresses. In my opinion, I'm too old to be wearing dresses to school. Pants are in style, bell-bottoms to be exact. To step into school wearing a pair of nylon bell-bottoms would be outta sight.

"You such a skinny little thing. Let's try on a size ten," Miz Lula Maye said as she looked through a rack full of ugly dresses. She didn't see me frowning 'cause I walked ahead of her on the way to the dressing room. I wasn't interested in any dresses, at least not for wearing to school.

After we picked out some dresses, Miz Lula Maye said, "Now where do we have to go to find some pants?" I couldn't believe it. I sho' was glad I didn't complain to Miz Lula Maye 'bout the dresses.

Miz Lula Maye is the bestest friend in the whole wide world. I ended up with two pairs of bell-bottoms, plus two pairs of jeans. Know what that means? I have to wear a dress at least one day out of the week. That's okay. I was just so, so happy to have four new pairs of pants.

We spent the whole day at Myrtle Beach, in and out of shops. For supper, we stopped at a restaurant that served mainly pizza. Pizza is "young folk's food," according to Miz Lula Maye. She didn't order pizza, but I sho' did. I ordered sausage with extra cheese, and it was gooood. Jack Jr. and Miz Lula Maye ordered fish-'n-chips. I guess fish-'n-chips is "grown-up folk's food."

The sun was setting when we walked back to the car. Everything sparkled and flashed like a treasure chest filled with magical jewels. The Ferris wheel was the most beautiful treasure of all. It was all lit up. Bright yellow, pink, blue, and green spun 'round and 'round. People were goin' in circles, screamin' and laughin' with their friends. When they got to the top of the wheel, they raised their hands high over their heads and cheered.

I wanted to be up there so bad. I wanted to be up there with my bestest friend, Miz Lula Maye. "Miz Lula Maye!" I said.

"Yes, child?" Miz Lula Maye answered. I could tell she was tired, so I thought twice about opening my mouth. I looked up at the Ferris wheel again. It was probably prettier from the ground, I decided. If you was ridin' it, you wouldn't be able to see all of its lights.

"I just wanted to say that this was probably one of the best days I ever had," I said.

"I'm glad, Sylvia," said Miz Lula Maye. She looked happy.

When we pulled out onto the highway, I couldn't see the lights of Myrtle Beach no more. I stretched out across the backseat and looked out the side window upside down. My eyes felt dry and heavy. I think the salty air probably dried out the liquid stuff in my eyes. That or either I was just plain old downright sleepy and tired. I looked out at the twinkling stars in the night sky. I was probably smilin' when I fell asleep.

Chapter  THREE

Rainy Day

The next morning, I woke up to heavy downpours of rain. It was raining cats and dogs. Miz Lula Maye and I watched more TV on this day than we'd watched all summer.

By afternoon, it rained even harder. It rained hogs and frogs. It rained so much til it made the day seem longer. Momma not calling made the day seem triple long and gloomy.

When I got tired of watching TV, I decided to go into my temporary bedroom. It's the room I always take when I spends the night at Miz Lula Maye's. Only difference is that now it was mine for as long as Momma was in Florida. Normally,

I'd be jumpin' for joy to have the chance of spending the night at Miz Lula Maye's. But now that I had nowhere else to stay, it just didn't seem to be as exciting. It wasn't like spending the night away from home.

I sat down on the bed and looked around as if I'd never seen the walls. Now Miz Lula Maye's house is my home, I thought. Everything looked different and felt different, too. I almost believed I felt nervous. My stomach felt like water in the toilet when it's being pulled and squeezed down into the hole. I didn't even think about Momma while I was at Myrtle Beach. Now, it seemed like Myrtle Beach was a dream. I was so happy. It was too perfect.

I hoped nothing bad had happened to Momma. She has had her share of bad luck. What if she's lost? I thought. What do grown-ups do anyhow when they gets lost? I was about to worry myself to pieces. Momma had probably met some of her folks and just hadn't gotten around to calling me (her one and only daughter), I told myself.

Things seemed really different. Usually when I feel this bad, I go get my white bunny rabbit that Momma gave me for Easter. I do that even though I'm almost eleven, 'cause sometimes that's what ya need. But I forgot to bring Bunny with me to Miz Lula Maye's house.

"Wait a minute!" I said kinda loud to myself. "I've got a key!" Momma gave me my very own key to our house, which is just down Pearle Road from Miz Lula Maye's. I jumped up and slid my ashy feet into my flip-flops.

The screen door slammed as I yelled out, "Miz Lula Maye, I'll be back in a minute!" Miz Lula Maye's raggedy old steps were drenched. It felt like I was waterskiing. I don't even remember my feet touching all of the steps.

I should've put on some real shoes. By the time I got halfway down Pearle Road, my feet was completely covered in gooey mud. My feet got so heavy, I had to stop runnin'. My entire body from head to toe was soaking wet. Momma would be mad if she saw me right now, I thought. And Miz Lula Maye, Lord knows I hope she ain't lookin' out her window.

When I made it to the house, I sat down on the back porch steps and stuck my feet out so the rain could rinse off the mud. My feet were like paintbrushes being rinsed off with water. The rain did a pretty good job.

I got really cold after my rain shower. I pulled the key out of my pocket and unlocked the door. It felt very strange going into my house and knowing that I was not gonna be stayin' there for a while. Also knowing that Momma was not gonna be there for a while either made the middle of my stomach ache.

Everything was just like we'd left it. Why wouldn't it be? I asked myself. Ghost could've moved things around, I answered like I was tryin' to scare myself. The house did seem spooky. It was sooo quiet. If there was a mouse, I would've heard it.

I walked into the front room. The pillow on the sofa was still wrinkled with Momma's head print. I made a quick check on the kitchen. The sink didn't have not one dirty dish. When I passed the bathroom, I could smell that new bar of Zest that I opened on Sunday. The fringes on Momma's rug in front of her bed were pulled in every-which-a-way. The closet door was missin'

Momma's black dressy handbag. I was missin' Momma, too. My eyes started burning.

I gave a big sigh that was extra loud in the quiet house. When I stopped sighing, I declare the sound of that sigh kept goin', like ahhhhhhh, like someone or something was breathin'.

"Who's that?" I said and looked around with my eyes as big as they could be. No one answered. "Time to get outta here!" I hollered.

Luckily, I was still thinkin' straight enough to remember why I came. I grabbed my bunny from my room and ran out the house as fast as I could run. My feet splished and splashed all the way back down muddy Pearle Road. I didn't look back 'cause I didn't want to know if that ghost was chasin' me.

I didn't notice it had stopped rainin' until I was almost back at Miz Lula Maye's house. That's when I started to feel silly. I was glad no one could see me. All I probably heard back at my house was myself breathing, I thought. I know there ain't no sucha thing as a ghost.

I looked up and saw all Miz Lula Maye's cats lined up and waiting on the porch. And they were lookin' at me like I was C-R-A-Z-Y. Did those cats move when I walked up the steps and sat down? Nope. Them is some boring cats. They sits on Miz Lula Maye's porch in the exact same spot all the time. It's just as if Miz Lula Maye has given them assigned seats.

Me, Bunny, and the cats sat there watching dozens of tiny bright green frogs hoppin' around all over the place. Mr. Window Cat pawed at a frog hopping near his window and almost fell off the sill. That was some kinda funny watching a cat lose its balance.

Mr. Window Cat got his name 'cause his assigned seat is on the windowsill. Back in Florida, I had assigned seats on my bus, in the cafeteria, at assemblies, and even on field trips. Everywhere you went, you had assigned seats. Everything was assigned, even the stupid hook for your coat and book bag.

I hate it when the teacher assigns seats. Teachers always end up putting you beside some-body you don't like. Hopefully, since Wakeview is so small, maybe they won't assign seats, I thought. What if I have to sit beside a nasty boy? Or some

prissy girl who thinks she's pretty or "Miss It?"

I was seriously starting to dread school. And the first day would be happenin' in less than twenty-four hours. I was so nervous, I felt like I could throw up, even though I'd done this before. We moved about three times in Florida. Everywhere I went was totally different, especially the kids. I reckon that's why I didn't hardly have no friends back in Florida. But things were different here, I reminded myself. Even if Momma wasn't here, I had a best friend. I had Miz Lula Maye.

Momma! What if Momma had been tryin' to reach me while I was actin' crazy in the rain? "Miz Lula Maye!" I yelled through the screen door. "Did Momma call?"

Miz Lula Maye came over to the door. "No, she didn't. Where you been? You took off so fast down the road. Is everything alright, baby?"

"Yes, ma'am," I answered, disappointed.

"Come on in here and get washed up. You know what tomorrow is? I'm gettin' excited like it's my first day of school."

Later in the evening, I got my school supplies

together for the first day at Fork Hollow Primary School. I also got all my school clothes out for the rest of the week. I never had those many clothes to choose from before.

I could feel Miz Lula Maye peekin' in on me every now and then. She really is the best friend and great-grandma in the whole wide world. Even my own momma doesn't know when to bother me and when to leave me alone. I guess maybe that's something you gotta learn. With Miz Lula Maye being a hundred, she ought to know. Probably when my momma gets older, she'll do better about knowing those kind of things.

Right before I went to bed, the phone rang. "Thank you, Jesus!" I yelled. "Yes! Yes! Yes! I bet it's my momma! Can I get it?"

"Go head, baby," said Miz Lula Maye. "You probably right."

Within a split second, I picked up the phone and said, "Hello?"

"Is that you, Sylvia?" said a voice.

I started jumpin' up and down and yellin', "It's Momma! It's her!" I probably hurt her ears, I yelled so loud.

"Momma, you'll never guess where we went on Monday!" I didn't give her a chance to answer. "We went to Myrtle Beach. Have you ever been there?"

"I've heard of Myrtle Beach, but I've never been," she said.

I told Momma all about Myrtle Beach. Then I told her about the rain. I even told her about the frogs. When I finally ran out of things to say, Momma said, "So you're okay, Sylvia?"

"Of course I'm okay," I answered. "I'm with Miz Lula Maye. Besides, I ain't no baby." Momma laughed. She said she was glad to hear me being my usual self.

Miz Lula Maye wanted to talk. I didn't want to give up the phone, but like a nice girl, I did. I had to be nosy. I didn't budge an inch from Miz Lula Maye's side. "It's been rainin' cats and dogs around here. I knows the catfish are biting up somethin' after all of this rain. . . . Sylvia has been doing just fine. Yes, indeed. She's a good girl and smart around the house, too," she said. Then Miz Lula Maye laughed, ca-cacka-cacka-cacka-cack.

I stood there beside Miz Lula Maye listening to her every words and grinning from ear to ear. I was as proud as could be to hear Miz Lula Maye bragging over me. It made me feel all warm inside, like hot fudge being poured over vanilla ice cream.

That night, I had the hardest time going off to sleep. I stared at the ceiling. Then I stared at the pictures on the wall. I tried to imagine what my first day of school would be like. Would the kids at Fork Hollow Primary School like me? Would I like them? What would my teacher be like?

Usually, man teachers are mean. They have to act that way so they can look tough and strong. Most of the time, man teachers teach math, history, and PE. My main teacher was gonna be a lady. Lady teachers are mean, too, I reminded myself. I don't know why. Most teachers are mean, probably 'cause they have to be. Well, maybe all teachers are not mean, just strict.

I don't remember fallin' asleep. I just remember worrying.

Sylvia Freeman

FOUR

Fork Hollow

Primary School

For the one-hundredth time, I read over my registration sheet.

Freeman, Sylvia F.
Grade 5 Year 1978–79
Room 403 Mrs. S. Harper
Fork Hollow Primary School
Wakeview, South Carolina

I wanted to make sure I had everything memorized. I also had to remember my bus number, which was 430. All I had to do was think of my favorite show, *Good Times*. It comes on TV at

4:30. So if I remembered that, I didn't think I'd be forgetting my bus number at all.

I took a bath the night before, so all I had to do was jump right into my brand-new clothes. I made a deal with Miz Lula Maye that I would wear a dress on the first day of school.

I decided on a blue jean romper dress with a big long silver zipper straight down the middle. The metal silver zipper-pull was shaped like a flower, a daisy. To me, that's what made this dress so pretty. Wearin' this dress to school wasn't gonna be so bad, I thought.

Miz Lula Maye could tell I was feeling nervous. "What you want to eat for breakfast this mornin'?" she asked.

I shrugged my shoulders and said, "Nothin'. I'm not very hungry."

"Childs, you know you gots to eat somethin'. It'll be hours before you gets to eat lunch," Miz Lula Maye said. Then she began spreading butter and sprinkling sugar over a few pieces of light bread.

Miz Lula Maye was all full of smiles. Did that mean she was ready to get rid of me? I wondered.

I hoped not, 'cause I was gonna miss her an awful bit of something. I was gonna miss hanging out with her, learning stuff and keepin' her company all day.

I reckoned the last person Miz Lula Maye sent to school from her house was my daddy. That's 'cause Miz Lula Maye raised my daddy after his momma died.

"Miz Lula Maye," I said, "do you remember when my daddy went to fifth grade?"

Miz Lula Maye said, "Oh, childs, that's been so long ago. I don't recollect his primary years, but I does remember him going to high school."

Miz Lula Maye stopped talking for a moment to pull the sugar toast from the oven. Then she chuckled, shaking her head from side to side. "I remember one time, I believes it was the year your daddy graduated from high school. . . ."

Oh boy, I thought. Is there time for one of Miz Lula Maye's stories? I started eating my sugar toast and tried not to think about the bus.

Miz Lula Maye went on. "Normally, the farm childrens 'round here takes into school later than the other kids. You know, the city kids. The kids from in town. The farm kids had to work puttin' in tobacco well after Labor Day.

"Well, your daddy had gathered in his head that he wasn't gonna help put in tobacco his senior year of schoolin'. So he'd take off for school extra early, knowing good 'n well he was needed in the fields. He'd rush home from school, head straight for the fields, and work til dark, twice as hard and twice as fast.

"After I saw what you daddy was doin' and I saw how serious he was about gettin' his schoolwork, I knew he was gonna be college material. So we hired an extra hand and let Jon Jon go on to gettin' his schoolin' early along with the city childrens."

Miz Lula Maye threw her hands up in the air and let out a loud laugh. She was some kinda tickled about something.

"Sylvia, Lord knows I sho' do remember the summer before your daddy went to that fine college. In Georgia? I believe that's right." Miz Lula Maye paused for a few seconds as if she wasn't quite sure.

This was all very interesting, but I was scared

I would miss my bus. I slowly leaned over to the side to try to see the clock behind Miz Lula Maye's head. "Sylvia, he practically near worked himself to death that summer. And do you know why?" she asked.

I snapped up straight again. "Why, Miz Lula Maye?"

Miz Lula Maye pinched at my cheeks. "Sylvia, childs, money don't grow on trees. Wish it did, but you know for yourself how hard your momma works. Colored folks 'round here has always had to work extra hard to get anyplace. Me and your daddy made a deal. I agreed to pay for his college tuition, and he paid for his books, food, clothes, and whatever else he wanted. So in other words, your daddy did what he had to do to go to college.

"I was so proud of him goin' off to that college." Miz Lula Maye put her arms around me and gave me a big hug. "I'm proud of you, too, going to school and all. I already knows you're some kinda smart. You gonna have a mighty good year of schoolin', Little Miss Sylvia. A mighty good year. Yes, indeed!"

Miz Lula Maye had me all pumped up and

ready to take on the first day of school like a heavyweight champion of the world. Only thing is, there ain't no girl boxers. At least, none that I've ever heard about. Who knows? One day there might be girls boxing in a ring like tough guys. I might become the first girl version of George Foreman.

I heard a loud horn sound from outside. "Oh, no!" I said. "It's the bus!" I ran to the window to see for sure if there really was a long yellow bus sittin' in the middle of Pearle Road.

"Sho' nuff!" said Miz Lula Maye. "That's your ride, Sylvia! It's time to go to school. Now hurry, child. Can't keep Mr. Knuckles waitin'."

I looked at Miz Lula Maye. I'm sure I had fright stuck all over my face like a big popped bubble of pink bubble gum. Bomp! Bomp! The horn honked again.

"Did you say Knuckles? Mr. Knuckles?" I asked. "What kind of name is that? Is that his real name or is it just a name ya'll folks 'round here made up?" I was stalling big time. All of a sudden, I was ready to sit down and listen to Miz Lula Maye tell me stories all day long.

Miz Lula Maye knew what I was up to. She put her arm around me and pushed me out the door. Straight ahead down Pearle Road, Miz Lula Maye escorted me to bus number 430. That was the first time Miz Lula Maye ever rushed me out of her house. It made me feel like pokin' my bottom lip out like a first grader.

I was already missin' Miz Lula Maye before I even sat down on the bus. I waved good-bye out the window like I was going on a long trip somewhere. Then Mr. Knuckles bomped his horn one more time and backed down Pearle Road.

Before I knew it, we were at school. A sign in front said "Fork Hollow Primary School, Home of the Hornets." I got off the bus and followed the other kids through the front door.

All of a sudden, I forgot everything that had been written on my registration sheet. Well, almost everything. I still knew my name was Sylvia, but I don't know if I could have been too sure about the year right then.

My room number is 430, I told myself. No, hold on, that was my bus number. My room number is 304. No, that wasn't right, either. My heart was pounding and I couldn't think. I'd only been at school for five minutes and I was already lost. I didn't know what to do.

"Snap out of it, girl!" I said.

I looked around quickly to make sure nobody was paying me any mind. I needed to stop talking out loud to myself. Folks might think I was not quite right in the head. Instead of being from Florida, folks might think I was from the funny farm.

Unfortunately, someone was looking at me. And even more undyn-o-mite, it was Taylor Jones. He was comin' waltzin' down the hallway like somebody important. Looked like he was floating in midair, the smooth way he was walkin'.

"Hey, Sylvia. Right?" said Taylor Jones, real cool, as if he wasn't sure whether or not if he remembered my name.

I could be cool, too. "Taylor. Right?" I said. This was ridiculous. We both knew we remembered each other perfectly fine from this summer at church. Who could forget TJ, who bites at my everlasting nerves every time I see him?

"So, who'd ya get?" asked Taylor Jones.

"What?" I asked, not knowing what on earth he was talkin' about.

"Who is your teacher?" he said.

Suddenly, I could remember one thing on the card. "S. Harper!" I said. "My teacher is Mrs. S. Harper!"

Taylor Jones looked at me like he wondered why that was so excitin'. Then he turned and motioned for me to come on. Like a puppy, I followed. Not in a million years was I gonna let Taylor Jones know that I was lost and scared to death.

When we got to room 403, I politely smiled and said, "Thanks, TJ." Then I realized what I said. I only call Taylor Jones "TJ" in my head. And now I had said it out loud. Taylor Jones just looked at me and grinned without sayin' one cotton-pickin' word. Then he turned and walked into the room. He left me hangin' like tobacco on a stick.

When I walked into the room, Mrs. S. Harper said, "Hello! You must be new to this school." She had a very pleasant and polite-sounding voice.

I said, "Yes, ma'am. I'm new to Wakeview. I came from Florida, at the beginning of the summer."

I was so nervous. Even more nervous than I thought I'd be. I think talkin' with Taylor Jones added to my nerves. I had no idea he'd be going to my school, not to mention in my class.

Just like I thought, we had assigned seats. Mrs. S. Harper had our names written so pretty on notecards with rainbows. When I found my desk, I looked at the names around me. They were all girl names. Thank goodness, I didn't have to be bothered with any boys sittin' too close to me, buggin' me for this and buggin' me for that.

I wondered what the S stood for in my new teacher's name. I guessed I'd find out sooner or later. Mrs. Harper said the theme for the first day of school was Getting to Know You. We played name games and memory games all day. So far, Mrs. Harper was a very nice teacher. Hopefully, she wouldn't turn into a witch like some of my teachers back in Florida, I thought. After the first month of school is over, the magic potion wears off.

The kids didn't seem much different than kids

in Florida. I never thought I would say this, but I was glad we had assigned seats at lunch. I talked to some of the girls in my class. I thought we might become friends, but I didn't know. At recess I waited for someone to come over and play with me, but nobody came.

Chapter FIVE

The

Friends Department

After two weeks and three days of school, I still didn't know what the S stood for in Mrs. S. Harper's name. But without a doubt, the H definitely stood for homework. I'd already had more homework than I had last year around Christmas.

I thought that maybe by now I would've become friends with some of the girls. But even though we talked a little at lunch, none of them seemed to really like me. I could just tell by the way they mostly had conversations with each other that usually didn't include me. Especially Stella and Leola.

Stella and Leola are what Miz Lula Maye calls "sometimey." Sometimes they acts like they know you, and sometimes they acts like they don't. All of Miz Lula Maye's cats are sometimey. (But she'd be ready to fuss with me if she knew I was sayin' that about her babies.)

At lunch Stella and Leola were talking about some songs they heard on *Soul Train*. "Freak out!" I heard Leola sing.

"I know, girl, it's gonna be the number one song on the charts. I can feel it in my bones," Stella said.

"Yeah, I like that song, too," I said, tryin' to put myself in the conversation.

Well, it was like I wasn't even there. Stella and Leola didn't even look at me. I tried again. "Do y'all know who it's by?" I asked, even though I already knew. I still can't believe it, but they switched topics just so they didn't have to answer my question.

I was so mad. I wanted to say, "I bet you switched the topic because you's too dumb and didn't know the answer." But I held my tongue.

I didn't understand what was goin' on in the

friends department. I was trying so hard to be extra super nice, but it wasn't working. Back in Florida, I definitely didn't put up with other people's AT-TI-TUDES. I had a lot of mouth back there, and I wasn't afraid to speak up. I didn't have a lot of friends, but I had a few. More than I had here, anyway.

The next day, we had a Welcome Back to School assembly in the auditorium. Stella, Leola, and Big Head Taylor Jones sat in the row behind me. I didn't like it one bit. I could hear them saying things, and I was pretty sure they was talkin' about me.

But after the assembly, Stella passed me a note. If someone gives you a note, it means they wants to be your friend. It looked like this bein' nice thing was finally working.

"Thanks," I said grabbing the note. Stella and Leola burst out laughing. I didn't know what was so funny, but I was too excited to pay it much mind.

The note was folded in a really neat triangle. I unfolded it on the way back to the classroom. Turned out it wasn't a note. It was a picture. It

was a stupid drawing of an old lady with a broom. She was wearing a witch hat. She was also surrounded by cats. I knew right away it was supposed to be Miz Lula Maye.

When I sat down at my desk, Stella, Leola, and Taylor Jones entered the classroom. I couldn't say a word. I couldn't even look at nobody. I figured the whole class probably knew about the note. I felt smaller than a worrisome gnat. For the first time in my entire life, I was being picked on.

I thought about the note all the way home to Pearle Road. I checked the mailboxes when I got off the bus. Then I decided to sit on my back porch steps before heading down to Miz Lula Maye's. Normally, I'd nosy through the mail, but my mind was totally occupied with that hateful non-note of a picture. I was so mad, I didn't even know what to do about it. How could they be that mean to Miz Lula Maye?

Finally, I walked down Pearle Road with my head stuck in the mud. I wished my momma was home. I didn't feel right goin' to Miz Lula Maye's house after lookin' at that picture.

Miz Lula Maye was waiting behind the screen

door as I crept up the steps. "Looks like you done and lost ya best friend. What's the matter, baby?"

"Nothing," I answered as if it was my last breath. "Nothin', I guess," I repeated, louder this time 'cause I knew Miz Lula Maye wasn't gonna let me rest. I walked into the kitchen and placed the mail on the table.

"You hungry?" Miz Lula Maye asked.

"Nah," I said.

"Thirsty?"

"I guess," I said.

Miz Lula Maye poured a glass of iced tea. I decided to pretend that I had homework. For a minute, I thought I was off the hook, but Miz Lula Maye doesn't let you get away with what she calls "half answers."

"Now, Sylvia, maybe I ain't been knowing you for years, but I wasn't born yesterday, either," she said. "I can tell somethin' is weighing on your mind."

I was startin' to get a little nerved with Miz Lula Maye. Why didn't she just leave me alone to do my homework, even if I really didn't have any?

"Did somethin' happen at school today?" she

asked. I didn't answer. There was no way in the world I could tell Miz Lula Maye about what happened.

"Well, I reckons you'll tell me when you gets ready," Miz Lula Maye said. She sat the glass of iced tea in front of me and went in the front room.

I got up and peeked through the door. Miz Lula Maye was sittin' in her chair and she was talkin' to her cats. "She probably had a bad day. We all has 'em every now and then," she said.

Miz Lula Maye musta taken a nap that afternoon 'cause her white hair was stickin' out on the sides. She was surrounded by five or maybe more cats. And that wasn't even all of them. For just a second, she kinda looked a little like the drawing. And for some reason, that made me even more nerved at her.

I was mad at everybody at school, especially Stella, Leola, and Big Head Taylor Jones. I was mad at Miz Lula Maye and her cats, and I was mad at me, Sylvia, for bein' mad. Oh, and Momma 'cause she wasn't there. Lord, I thought, I can't be mad at you, but I feels like I should. I didn't know who to blame.

Miz Lula Maye was still talkin' to her cats. "I know what might perk up Sylvia," she said, and she popped up out of her chair.

I sat down at the table again real quick. Every time she moves fast like that, like somebody young, it scares me. People her age ought to move slow.

"Sylvia, baby, your birthday is comin'. Why don't we have a birthday party?" said Miz Lula Maye. "You could invite some of your new friends from school." I almost knocked over my glass of tea.

Usually, Miz Lula Maye does know what would make me feel better. But this time, she got it dead wrong. I didn't have any new friends from school to invite. Thanks the Lord, Jack Jr. came walkin' in the house as if it was time to eat. "What's goin' on?" he asked.

"We were just plannin' Sylvia's birthday party," said Miz Lula Maye.

"Dyn-o-mite!" said Jack Jr. "Can I come?"

I've heard folks in Wakeview thinks Jack Jr. is not wrapped too tight. It's true, he ain't. When I tried to picture Stella and Leola at a birthday party with Jack Jr., I was terrified with even the thought. That would be the worst thing.

Jack Jr. and Miz Lula Maye were lookin' at me kind of funny. I had to come up with something quick. "Um, I don't really want a party," I said. "I mean, I like birthdays, but I'm kinda busy this year with startin' at a new school 'n all." I made my eyes wide and smiled real big so they knew that I was really very happy about this idea.

"Alright, Sylvia," said Miz Lula Maye. "If you don't have time for a birthday this year, we'll just celebrate twice as big next year."

What had I done? I didn't mean I didn't want any birthday. I just didn't want a birthday party. But it was too late. I had just canceled my own birthday.

Friday, September 29, was the day that was supposed to be my eleventh birthday. Momma called me before school to say happy birthday, 'cause she didn't know it wasn't happy or birthday. Miz Lula Maye watched TV all night long on the night that wasn't my birthday anymore. I was supposed to be busy, so I couldn't even watch it with her. And of course, Jack Jr. was at the Juke Joint.

The Juke Joint was Jack Jr.'s club. It was across Pearle Road from the house where Momma and I lived. Every Friday evening, the Juke Joint was the hoppin'est place in South Carolina and North Carolina. Saturday, too.

On Sunday, I was still feelin' pretty bad about missing my birthday. Around six o'clock, Jack Jr. dropped by the house. "You wanna start earning a little change by helpin' out at the Juke Joint?" he asked. "I need someone to restock the snacks."

"How much change you talkin'?" I asked.

"Listen at Sylvia, Auntie Maye," Jack Jr. said. "She's tryin' to sound like she knows a little somethin' about money. How does two dollars sound?"

I thought about it for a quick moment. Working at the Juke Joint sounded better than sittin' around thinking about my birthday. "Okay, that sounds pretty good," I said.

Miz Lula Maye gave me a long look. "You sure you not too busy, Sylvia?" she asked.

"No, ma'am," I said.

"Well, I might as well come, too. Ya'll wait for me to slip on a jacket. I ain't been up to the Juke Joint in a week or two," said Miz Lula Maye.

The first thing I noticed when I walked into the Juke Joint was a white box sitting in the middle of a table. "What's this?" I asked.

"Open it and see," said Jack Jr.

I quickly ripped off the one piece of tape stuck on the lid of the box. Inside was the most beautiful birthday cake I had ever seen. It looked like something for a princess. It had white frosting and big pink and lavender flowers. "Happy Birthday Sylvia" was written across the top of the cake in dark purple. My eyes felt blurry and wet. I was gettin' a birthday after all.

Turns out there were gifts, too. Momma gave me a pair of real 14-carat gold earrings. "But my ears ain't pierced," I complained.

"Your momma wants to take you to the beauty parlor when she gets back," said Miz Lula Maye.

"For real?" I asked. I couldn't believe it.

"It's gonna hurt til Christmas," teased Jack Jr.

"Hush yo' mouth," Miz Lula Maye warned him.

"Is it really gonna hurt?" I asked. "Maybe I should wait."

Miz Lula Maye put her arm across my back. "Don't pay him no mind. It'll be a quick pinch, over and done in a flash."

Miz Lula Maye gave me a diary. "All my girls had diaries when they was eleven," she remembered. My daddy had sent me a blue jean pocketbook with a matching wallet from up North, which is where he lives. The wallet had eleven dollars in it ('cause it was my eleventh birthday), plus four quarters for good luck.

Jack Jr. was too lazy to buy me a gift. He claimed he didn't know what I'd like. Maybe that's true. I shouldn't complain. He gave me a five dollar bill. It ended up being the perfect gift 'cause it went right into my new wallet.

If Momma had been there, the party would have been perfect. Not having Momma around for my birthday felt weird. I don't know my daddy too well, but I guess it would've been nice to have him come, too. But like Miz Lula Maye keeps reminding me, nothin' in life is ever gonna be completely perfect. You gotta just enjoy life however it comes. So I did just that, and my belated birthday ended up bein' happy.

Chapter SIX

Contests

A week after my birthday, Momma called again. She talked to me a little bit, but mostly she talked to Miz Lula Maye. They talked a long time. I hung around so I could figure out what was goin' on.

Miz Lula Maye was sayin' things like, "Well, isn't that nice" and "It's no trouble at all" and "You do what you need to do."

When she finally hung up the phone, I was about ready to bust. "What's happenin', Miz Lula Maye? Tell me. I can tell somethin' is up."

Miz Lula Maye explained that Momma had found some of her relatives, which is very lucky 'cause Momma always figured she didn't have nobody left. She was staying with her second cousins, Miz Adair and Mr. Patrick. They owned a flower business called Adair's Florist.

"Your momma has decided to stay down there a little longer," said Miz Lula Maye.

"What?" I said. "But she's supposed to be comin' home soon. What about gettin' my ears pierced? Why doesn't she want to come home?"

"Don't worry, child, your Momma is comin' home. But first she's going to learn how to make flower arrangements," said Miz Lula Maye. "Your momma is young. Naturally, she ought to be discoverin' new things. I thinks learning how to make flower arrangements sounds mighty fine. Don't you think so, Sylvia?"

At first I didn't say nothin'. No one told me Momma would be gone for so long. Miz Lula Maye just sat there and waited for me to answer her question.

Finally I said, "Momma has always taken a liking to flowers. Maybe she can teach us when she gets back."

Miz Lula Maye gave me a big squeeze. "Yes, indeed," she said. "I might be a hundred, but there's still more for me to learn."

I probably would've worried more about Momma bein' gone if I didn't get the news I got on Monday at school.

"Class, please settle down," said Mrs. Harper after lunch. "It's time to talk about the Wakeview Fall Carnival."

I didn't know nothin' about any fall carnival, so I looked very carefully at the paper she passed out. On the front was a list of events. The back of the paper was even more interesting. There was gonna be contests at the carnival.

I didn't even read the list of contests 'cause right away my eyes went to one of them. "Poetry Contest," it said.

Back in Florida, I used to write poems all the time. Usually, I writes when I'm bored. I hadn't written a word since I'd been here in Wakeview 'cause I'd been too busy with Miz Lula Maye. Havin' a best friend really cuts down on your bored time.

"As you probably know, the carnival will begin a week from this Friday and will run through Sunday," explained Mrs. Harper. "I especially want to encourage you to enter the poetry contest, which I will be in charge of this year. The poems are due next Monday."

Mrs. Harper told us that the top ten best poems would be read at the carnival before the winners were announced.

Everybody started talking about the carnival. "Man, the bumper cars always plays the best music," said Jason.

"Last year the music was blastin' so loud it shook the floor," Taylor Jones said. Then he saw me lookin' at him, and he smiled his wacko smile at me. I turned around, shut my eyes, and imagined myself accepting the first-place prize in the poetry contest.

"Sylvia, that poetry contest sounds interesting, doesn't it?" said a quiet voice.

I opened my eyes. A girl named Belinda was lookin' at me. I glanced around to make sure it was Belinda talking to me 'cause she never talks. She's usually quieter than a mouse.

"I think so," I said. "Are you going to enter?"

Belinda nodded. "Do you want to work together?" she asked. Her voice was so quiet, I wasn't sure I heard her right.

"You want to work with me?" I asked. Belinda nodded again.

We decided to sit together at lunch the next day and talk some more. I was excited. I figured it was a good chance that Belinda and I may become friends. Why? Because we'd both been in the same boat as far as the friends department was concerned. Meanwhile, I had just one week to write a really good poem. What about? I had no idea.

My bus ride home from school didn't seem to exist. I had so much on my mind, I didn't notice time. When my bus stopped on Pearle Road, I noticed Jack Jr. sweeping the walkway to the Juke Joint.

I ran up to him yelling, "It's carnival time!"

"Sure is," said Jack Jr. "Why don't you come help me restock the freezer, Cousin Sylvia."

"That's a cold job!" I complained.

"Who you tellin'? I'm the one who normally does it, and by myself, too," he said.

I filled the freezer with orange and strawberry soda pop. Jack Jr. stacked boxes of ice cream sandwiches, Fudgsicles, and Nutty Buddies in the brrr section of the freezer.

"Are you gonna enter any of the contests at the carnival?" Jack Jr. asked.

"Maybe," I said.

"Let's see, now," said Jack Jr. "there's all kinds of cooking and canning contests. There's contests for the best farm animals, like the heaviest hog, the biggest Black Angus, and the tallest rooster. Oh, and the vegetable-growing contests, like the biggest watermelon and pumpkin, the longest squash, the biggest tomato, the widest collard leaves, and the heaviest onion."

"So which ones are you gonna enter?" I asked.

"Not a cotton-pickin' one of 'em," replied Jack Jr. "Contests is for show-offs."

When I didn't say anything, Jack Jr. said, "Sylvia, I's joking withs ya. Which ones are you going to enter? Spit it out. Don't be shame."

"The poetry one," I said and put the last bottle in the freezer. I waited for a silly comment to escape from Jack Jr.'s mouth.

Surprisingly, he didn't make a wisecrack about me entering the poetry contest. Maybe he has a little more sense than I thought.

"The poetry contest. Well, that's fine."

"Hey, can I have a Nutty Buddy to go?" I asked.

Jack Jr. looked at me and smiled. "Get you one. That's the least I can do. To go? Where you headed?"

"Home to Miz Lula Maye's," I answered.

"Hold on for a second. I'll walk with ya."

Even in the fall, Wakeview has gnats. I guess they has 'em year-round. I ate my Nutty Buddy as we walked down Pearle Road fanning gnats, mosquitoes, horseflies, and every other insect on the planet.

Miz Lula Maye's cats were all lined up on her porch. They didn't care if they was in the way or not.

"Get, get, get out of here!" said Jack Jr. when he almost tripped over Miz Basket Cat. "Get off a this here porch!"

Miz Lula Maye appeared in the screen door like magic. "How you doin', Sylvia? I ain't speaking to crazy folks who holler at cats that mind their own business."

I laughed so hard at Miz Lula Maye's comment that the Nutty Buddy I'd just finished eating almost came back up.

The next morning, I got my second note at Fork Hollow Primary School. Only this time, it really was a note. It said:

Sylvia,

Do you think I could come over to your house after school tomorrow so we can work on our poems?

Write back,
Belinda

At first, I was so excited. But then I started thinking. What would Belinda think about Miz Lula Maye? What if she thought she looked like a witch, too? And what if Jack Jr. did something embarrassing? Belinda would never want to be my friend after that. I had to make sure Belinda didn't come out to Pearle Road. But how?

I decided not to write back. All morning, I was afraid to look at Belinda. By lunchtime, I still hadn't figured out what to tell her. Belinda saved a place for me at lunch, but I pretended like I didn't see it. I sat way on the other side of the lunchroom.

By the time the bus dropped me off, my stomach felt sick and my head hurt from tryin' so hard not to look at Belinda. Pearle Road seemed to have grown by a couple of miles.

Miz Lula Maye lives in a farmhouse at the end of the road. The house is old, just like Miz Lula Maye. The boards could use new paint, and the screens on the windows had a few rips. All the houses on Pearle Road are in the same shape on the outside. They never bothered me before. But now I wished Miz Lula Maye would fix up the place. Folks probably think we're dirt poor, lazy, or just downright too cheap to get things like new, I thought as I trudged down the road.

When I got home, Jack Jr. was in the kitchen with Miz Lula Maye. "Auntie Maye," he said, "when you gonna ask Sylvia to be in the costume contest with you?"

"What costume contest?" I asked.

"At the carnival," said Jack Jr. "I told you about it."

"You told me about a hog contest and a pumpkin contest. You didn't say nothin' about no costume contest," I said.

"Well, Sylvia, now that Jack has done and ready told you what I was gonna ask you, what do you think about it?" asked Miz Lula Maye.

"What would we be?" I asked.

"I was thinking angels, if that's alright with you," said Miz Lula Maye. "We can make the costumes. It'll be fun! I've already got some old white choir robes. The only thing we needs to make are wings and halos."

Angels? Twin angels? I was horrified. This was not a dyn-o-mite idea. But Miz Lula Maye and Jack Jr. were lookin' at me with big smiles on their faces, so I said, "Sure! I think that would be great!"

While I was smilin' back at them, I was praying in my mind, "Lord, please help me. I don't want no one from school to see me and Miz Lula Maye dressed up like angels." But I knew that the chance that no one would see us was exactly zero.

Chapter

SEVEN

The Stinkin'

Grocery Store

I didn't talk to Belinda all week. After I ignored
her note, she started ignoring me. That had to be
one of the shortest friendships ever known. Miz
Lula Maye kept asking me if I wanted to work on
our angel costumes. I told her I was too busy, but
the costume contest kept getting closer and
closer.

Speakin' of contests, I was supposed to have a
poem ready on Monday, and by Saturday I didn't
have the first word written down.

I sat in my room all Saturday morning, staring
at a blank piece of paper. When I'm just goofin'
off, rhymes come out like mosquitoes on a late

summer night. Usually, it's like natural and auto-matic. But it wasn't now.

After lunch, Miz Lula Maye became busier than a bee. She grabbed a couple of brown paper grocery bags with *Reaves* written in red across the front. Jack Jr. takes Miz Lula Maye to do her grocery shoppin' at Reaves Supermarket in downtown Wakeview. At Reaves Supermarket, if you bring their bags back, they gives you a discount off your grocery bill.

"Come on, Sylvia! Let's walk over to Jack's," Miz Lula Maye said. "I needs to see if he can take us to Reaves so I can shop for my carnival baking." She wasted no time shuttin' up the house and heading for the front door.

"But Miz Lula Maye, wait," I said. "I can't go into town. I have to work on writing my poem for the poetry contest. It's no fair. They didn't give us enough time!"

"Sylvia, now you quit your complainin' and come on," said Miz Lula Maye. "You have tonight and all day tomorrow to write that poem. Gettin' out this here house might help you come up with some ideas."

There was no use. Miz Lula Maye wouldn't take no for an answer.

"Gotcha grocery bags, I see," said Jack Jr. when he opened his door. "Auntie Maye, you needin' to go to Reaves?"

Miz Lula Maye said, "Yes, I needs to get my shoppin' out of the way today so I can start bakin' my pecan goodies for the carnival."

While Miz Lula Maye was talking, Jack Jr. was lookin' around as if he'd lost something. He was shakin' his hands in the front pockets of his pants. Next he moved his hands to check his back pockets. Then he jerked his hands to his chest and checked his shirt pockets. Finally, he held up a finger and scurried his way to his beat-up old raggedy car. His keys were still in the car.

"Let's go, ladies!" said Jack Jr.

At first, we was all so quiet that all you could hear was the bump, bump, bump of the tires over the road. Then Miz Lula Maye said, "Sylvia, did I ever tell you who planted all my pecan trees?"

"No, you didn't, Miz Lula Maye," I said, wonderin' why she was talkin' about pecan trees all of a sudden.

"Squirrels!" said Miz Lula Maye and then ca-cacka-cack, she laughed.

Did Miz Lula Maye really think that squirrels had planted her pecan trees? I wondered. I heard old folks get mixed up from time to time. They forgets stuff, too.

A girl in my class named Wanda says that her grandmother thinks she is always hearing something. Out of the blue, for no reason, she'll say, "Huh?" Wanda says it's just something you get used to and learn to ignore.

What if Miz Lula Maye starts to forgetting important things? I worried. What if she acts strange at the costume contest? Before I could say anything about the squirrels, we pulled into the parking lot of Reaves Supermarket.

I'd never been grocery shoppin' with Miz Lula Maye before. When I walked in the door, a strange smell hit me in the face. I think it was part raw meat and part fresh collard greens, which don't smell good unless they's cooked and ready to eat. You talkin' about something that stinks, if you put collard greens in the 'frigerator and keep 'em too many days, it smells like a dead rat. A dead, decayed rat in hot weather is the worst smell on earth.

I pinched my nose for a long time, until my nose started hurting. Thank goodness, the smell didn't bother me too bad after a couple of minutes.

Miz Lula Maye let me push the cart. She would point to what she needed, and I'd fetch it from the shelves. We filled that shoppin' cart with lots of flour, table sugar, powered sugar, real butter, vanilla flavoring, molasses, syrup, chocolate squares, and waxed paper.

For the first time in days, I was havin' fun. I liked drivin' the cart. I pretended I was drivin' a car. I zoomed past the cereal and made a turn at the end of the aisle and headed for the eggs. The only thing missin' was a horn so people would get out of my way. I came to a quick stop behind Miz Lula Maye.

"Settle down, child!" she said. "I don't want you runnin' over anything. Especially the back of my heels."

Miz Lula Maye bought lots of eggs, both white and brown. She says that brown eggs is perfect

for baking things, especially if you wants your food to taste buttery.

"White eggs is good for breakfast eatin' and addin' to casseroles and dinner dishes. But brown eggs, they's some kinda good in desserts," said Miz Lula Maye.

Something was missin' from the cart. "Ain't you gonna buy no pecans for your pecan goodies, Miz Lula Maye?" I asked.

"Child, you don't need to buy pecans when you got a yard full of pecan trees at home," said Miz Lula Maye.

"You gonna use your own pecans?" I said. "Well, allll right! A dyn-o-mite!" Miz Lula Maye shook her head and laughed.

Next we went through the meat department and I almost wished I'd stayed in the car with Jack Jr. I saw some disgusting stuff, blood 'n all— gross, gross, grosser! Ain't like I've never been to the grocery store and seen meat before. I just ain't never seen it whole, the meat still in the shape of the animal it came from.

First thing I saw was a pig's head decorated with green leaves and red tomatoes, with purple onions situated all around it. And it was dead! I couldn't believe my eyes. Pig feet and pig ears were packed in gray trays for people to buy.

"Who in the world wants to buy a pig's ears, let alone its nasty feet?" I asked.

Miz Lula Maye picked up something that looked like big noodles, but it was meat. And yes, of course, it did come from a pig.

"We ain't gonna eat that, are we?" I asked.

"Sho' we is!" said Miz Lula Maye. "These is the intestines from a pig. You ever had chitlins, Sylvia?" I was scared to death. I didn't answer. I'd be dead meat myself if I ate those meat noodles.

"I'm gonna use these to make some spicy chitlins," said Miz Lula Maye. "First, I'll wash 'em real good. Then I'll soak 'em and boil 'em in salt, pepper, celery, onions from my garden, and lots of my homemade hot sauce. Mmm! Mmm! I'm talkin' up an appetite. I sho' loves me some chitlins."

Well, I sho' ain't hungry, I thought, and I ain't never eatin' no chitlins today, tomorrow, or any day. Those were some nasty, slimy-lookin' things. Why would anybody want to eat the intestines of a pig? I guess only God knows and, well, maybe Miz Lula Maye.

And what took the cake at Reaves Supermarket? Miz Lula Maye picked up a pack of hog brains. When she put 'em in the grocery cart, I stepped back. I no longer had any interest in pushin' the cart. My mouth started tasting funny, nasty, bad, like I hadn't brushed my teeth in months. My stomach felt like it was trying to turn inside out. I knew I best head for the front door of Reaves Supermarket before I had a major accident. Didn't think I'd ever want to eat meat again.

On the way home, I asked Miz Lula Maye if she was really gonna use her own pecans in her baking. "Will there be enough, Miz Lula Maye?"

"Sho' will," she said. "I gots plenty of trees."

"How did you get so many pecan trees?" I asked.

"Long ago, I believes there was only about two trees," Miz Lula Maye explained. "The squirrels and other little critters likes to dig and store nuts. I've always reckoned they probably planted all these pecans trees up 'round here. Didn't happen overnight. Every year, a few more trees would pop up from out of the ground. I do declare it was kinda like magic. I knew I hadn't planted no pecan trees."

So the squirrels really did plant the trees. I felt bad for thinkin' there was something wrong with Miz Lula Maye. She may be one hundred years old, but she knows what she's talkin' about.

Jack Jr. carried the grocery bags into the house. I helped by carrying the bag with the eggs. Miz Lula Maye says that Jack Jr. is sometimes heavy-handed and that she didn't need him to crack not one egg.

I helped Miz Lula Maye put away the groceries so I didn't have to look at the blank piece of paper lying on my bed. I still didn't have a poem in mind. At this point, I wondered if Miz Lula Maye's cats could even come up with a better poem than I could.

Chapter  EIGHT

Me and My

Big Mouth

Even though I was running out of time to write my poem, I still had to go to church the next morning. Not going to church is unheard of in Miz Lula Maye's house unless you're sick.

At Sunday school, you-know-who had to be present. It's bad enough Taylor Jones was in my class at school. I had to see him Monday through Friday, plus Sunday at church. That only gave my nerves a one-day measly little break.

"Hey, Sylvia, did you sign up for the poetry contest?" asked TJ.

I looked at him like he was stupid. I hadn't talked to him since he and Stella and Leola sent me that evil note about Miz Lula Maye, so I didn't know why he was talking to me now. "Why you want to know?" I answered. "Did you sign up for the contest is the question."

"Of course I'm in. I won the contest last year, and I'm gonna win it again this year, too. Bet-cha didn't know that," said TJ with a foolish smirk written all over his face.

"Yeah? I entered, too," I said. "And I plan to win!" I looked at him directly in his face.

TJ looked at me and said, "Hah! Oh please, girl. Don't get your ham-hock hopes up too high. I can write, girl."

"Like that note that you sent me about Miz Lula Maye?" I said with my hands on my hips. "Well, if that's what you call writing, I'm not impressed!"

"What note?" said Taylor, looking confused.

"You know what note," I said. "The note that you and Stella and Leola gave me."

TJ shook his head. "I don't know nothin' about a note."

I didn't know whether to believe him or not. But of course, I had to have the last word. "Well,

I can write, too. I been writing poems ever since I learned to read and write." If I was still ten, I would've stuck out my tongue at him. I decided I was gonna call Taylor Jones Mr. Smarty Pants. He thought he knew everything. So Mr. Smarty Pants was a suitable name.

After a big Sunday dinner (without any pig parts, thank you, Jesus), Miz Lula Maye, Jack Jr., and I sat on the front porch. I tried to work on my poem. Miz Lula Maye was humming, nodding her head as if she was still listening to the gospel choir sing. "Pastor really preached this morning," she said.

"Auntie Maye, you say the same thing every Sunday. 'Pastor really preached,'" Jack Jr. said, imitating Miz Lula Maye.

Any other time or day their fussin' would have been funny. But today, they kept fussin' back and forth til they got on my nerves. Before I could stop myself I said, "Stop, you two! You know I'm tryin' to write a poem!"

Jack Jr. and Miz Lula Maye stopped. Then they (including about seven cats) looked at me like I was completely cuckoo.

"Oh, excuse us," Jack Jr. smirked. "We better hush up, Auntie Maye, before Sylvia gets after us with a switch." I was really mad. And listening to Jack Jr. and his smart remarks made me madder.

"Why don't you just write a roses are red, violets are blue type of poem?" Jack Jr. said, as if he knew something about writing poetry. "Listen to this, Cousin Sylvia. Roses are red, violets aren't pink. I think that's the reason why your breath stink."

My mouth is usually what gets me in trouble. Did I care at the moment? No, not one bit with a capital NO. "Lord, if that's not the stupidest poem I ever heard, I don't know what is," I said. I gathered my pencil and blank sheet of paper and walked into the house.

I could hear Miz Lula Maye laughing along with Jack Jr. That really hurt my feelings. I went to my room and threw my pencil and paper on the floor. I had to get outta there. I yanked Bunny off my bed and stomped all the way back to the porch. Some cats were sprawled out on the floor. I scared them on purpose by stomping my feet as hard as I could stomp.

"Where you goin'?" asked Jack Jr.

I should've kept on walking, but I didn't. I turned around and said way too much. "I'm goin' anywhere but here!" I yelled. I pointed my finger at Jack Jr. and Miz Lula Maye. "Ya'll the real reason why I ain't got no new friends at school. Everyone, even Belinda, treats me real standoffish."

Tears oozed out of my eyes. I couldn't believe I was doin' it, but I pointed my finger right at Miz Lula Maye. "Folks think you're weird living in this unpainted old house with a hundred cats!" I yelled. "And folks think I'm weird because I live here, too. And another thing, I don't want to be in some silly costume contest dressed up like an angel!"

Miz Lula Maye was lookin' at me with her mouth hangin' open like she didn't believe what she was hearin'. I took off running as fast as my feet would move.

I ran all the way down to the end of Pearle Road and finally came to a stop in front of the Juke Joint. I stood there gasping for air like a fish pulled out of Catfish Creek. I didn't know what to do. I didn't know where to go. I looked across the road at the house I shared with Momma. It didn't look scary anymore. It just looked empty and sad. Then I remembered that I was too busy runnin' from the ghost to lock the door behind me last time I was there.

I ran across Pearle Road, up the steps, and into my house. I shut the door tight behind me. I went into the kitchen and sat down at the table. Then I had nothin' left to do but think.

I wasn't mad anymore. I was more embarrassed and ashamed. Then I pictured the look on Miz Lula Maye's face when I was yellin' at her, and I don't even know what to call the feeling that made me feel. I bent over, wrapped my arms around my waist, and started to cry.

I finally had a real family and a real home and a real best friend, and I ruined it. I ruined everything. I ignored Belinda so she didn't want to be my friend. Jack Jr. was always funny and nice to me, and now he probably hated me. Worst of all, after what I said to Miz Lula Maye, there was no way she would be my best friend anymore. I was so mean, she probably wouldn't want to be my great-grandma, either.

I sat there for a long time 'cause I had nowhere else to go. I couldn't go back to Miz Lula Maye's house after what I said to her. I couldn't go back there ever. I figured I'd just have to stay alone in my empty house until Momma got back.

It was so quiet, I could hear it loud and clear when some feet walked up the steps to the house. The screen door opened, and I took off running and hid in Momma's bedroom closet.

"Sylvia, baby, it's alright," said Miz Lula Maye's voice. "We knows you in here."

"Sylvia, I'm sorry for cuttin' the fool withs ya," said Jack Jr's voice. "I was just teasin' you. Come on out. If you don't come out, Auntie Maye will blame me and say it's my fault that you're hiding."

I was so scared to talk to Jack Jr. and Miz Lula Maye that I panicked. "Leave me alone!" I yelled. "I want to stay in my own house. Now that I'm eleven, I'm old enough to live alone!"

Miz Lula Maye opened the closet door and looked down at me huddled on the floor. "No, baby. Eleven ain't old enough. Who told you that?"

Jack Jr. peeked over Miz Lula Maye's shoulder and said, "I'm leaving. I'll see y'all later." Then it was just me and Miz Lula Maye alone in the house. I knew I had to come out. I crawled out of the closet and stood up.

"Sylvia, baby, why are you hidin?" asked Miz Lula Maye.

"I don't know," I whispered looking at the floor.

"Well, let's go in the front room and have a girl-to-girl talk," Miz Lula Maye said reaching for my hand.

"Now first, I believes you owe me an apology. Then I'll owe you an apology," instructed Miz Lula Maye when we sat down.

"I'm sorry, Miz Lula Maye. I didn't mean to say those terrible things and yell at you 'n all," I said.

"I accepts your apology, Sylvia. And I'm sorry I laughed at you when you was havin' such a hard time," said Miz Lula Maye. "Now, tell me, baby, what's been bothering you? I won't get mad. I just want to understand things so I can help you."

I was so worn out from worrying that I finally told Miz Lula Maye everything. And I mean everything. "Nobody at school acts like they want to be my friend," I said. "When school started, I tried being very nice. But still the kids treated me kinda mean."

"Well, what 'n all did they do?" Miz Lula Maye asked in a serious voice.

I told Miz Lula Maye about the way the girls ignored me and didn't talk to me during lunch. And how sometimes they said things about me behind my back. And then I told Miz Lula Maye about the note that wasn't a note. By the time I finished describing the picture, I couldn't believe it, but Miz Lula Maye was laughing.

"What are you laughing at, Miz Lula Maye?" I asked. "That note was mean!"

"Yes, it was, child," said Miz Lula Maye, wiping her eyes 'cause she was laughing so hard. "And I'm sorry it hurt you. But I guess I've gotten a little particular in my old age."

"What's *particular*, Miz Lula Maye," I asked.

"Hmmm. I guess it means ya do things your own way," she said.

Now that Miz Lula Maye was laughing about the note, it didn't seem as bad. "Miz Lula Maye, can you be particular even if you is only eleven years old?"

"Well, I guess you can be," said Miz Lula Maye. "It's always a good thing to know who ya are. And when ya do, you'll get the kind of friends who like what they see when they look at you."

By this time, I was snuggled up under Miz Lula Maye on the sofa like a cat. "I was afraid you wouldn't want me to come back home after what I said," I told her.

"You're my family, child, and your home is with your family," said Miz Lula Maye. "The Lord knew what he was doing when he led your momma to Wakeview. We were all meant to be together. You and me, Sylvia, the Lord put us together." Miz Lula Maye threw her hands up, ready to shout. I mean shout and get happy like folks do in church when they's praisin' the Lord.

Sometimes when Miz Lula Maye gets all up in the air about the goodness of the Lord, it feels like there's a nice cold piece of red cherry freeze pop sliding down my throat when it's raw from coughing or when I've had a bad cold. That's a nice soothing and good feeling. It's the kind I get when Miz Lula Maye wraps her arms around me and squeezes.

"It's cold in here," said Miz Lula Maye. "Let's go home."

Before bedtime, I wrote a poem that I felt really good about. It came straight from my heart, and that's where Mrs. Harper says the best poems come from.

"Lord, please, please help me make it to the top ten," I prayed before I fell asleep. I'd never be able to face Mr. Smarty Pants Taylor Jones again if I didn't.

Chapter  NINE

Pecan

Goodies

Monday morning I woke up to the heavenly smell of buttermilk biscuits and bacon. I made up my bed and headed for the bathroom to wash up and brush my teeth.

I rinsed my mouth out three times. Sometimes toothpaste can leave a weird aftertaste. And I definitely didn't want any other taste in my mouth other than what Miz Lula Maye was cookin'.

The weather seemed a little dreary outside, but in the kitchen, things were warm and toasty. Miz Lula Maye was standin' at the sink. "What happens at the carnival if it rains?" I asked.

Miz Miz Lula Maye stopped what she was doing and reached for a towel to dry her hands. Then she turned around and said, "Mornin', Sylvia. Did you get a good night's sleep?"

"Oops! I'm sorry, Miz Lula Maye," I said. "Good morning! How are you feelin' this morning? The smell of your good cookin' woke me up a bit early."

Miz Lula Maye smiled. "I'm doin' fine, Sylvia. Thanks for askin'," she said. "Most of the carnival is under tents except the rides. So even if it rains, the carnival will still go on."

Oh boy! I thought. Rides, rides, rides. I wonder if they'll be anything close to like what I saw at Myrtle Beach? Taylor Jones sure seemed excited about the rides when Mrs. Harper announced the carnival, so they must be pretty good. Hold on. I shook my head from side to side. Why was I wastin' time thinkin' about Taylor Jones?

For some reason, I kept thinkin' about Big Head Taylor Jones the whole time I was eatin' breakfast. Finally, I couldn't hold it in anymore.

"Miz Lula Maye, Taylor Jones and I kinda got into a little argument at church yesterday. He said that he won the poetry contest last year and that he was gonna win it this year, too. He made me so mad. You do know Taylor Jones, Miz Lula Maye? He bites at my last nerves. I don't care where we are, he never fails to say something stupid or do something stupid to aggravate me. Why do boys do that?"

All the time while I was fussin' about Taylor Jones, Miz Lula Maye was smilin' at me. When I noticed and stopped fussin', I asked Miz Lula Maye, "What's so funny? Why you smilin' at me like that?"

Miz Lula Maye scratched behind her ear, "I'm smilin' 'cause you's smilin'."

I was totally confused. "But Miz Lula Maye, I was just fussin'," I protested.

Then Miz Lula Maye said, "True, that may be true you was fussin', but the whole time you was fussin', you was smilin', all gums."

I didn't know what to say. It was almost time to catch the bus, so I gathered my things. As I was headin' out the door, I turned around and said, "Miz Lula Maye, are you tryin' to say that I like Taylor Jones?"

"You's the only one who's sayin' anything about liking Taylor Jones," Miz Lula Maye said.

As I walked down Pearle Road to the bus stop, I could hear Miz Lula Maye laughin', right tickled over the whole Taylor Jones discussion.

By the time I got to my classroom, the only thing I had on my mind was the poetry contest. "Good morning, Mrs. Harper," I said and handed her my poem.

Mrs. Harper smiled a big, cheerful smile. "Thank you, Sylvia," she said. "I can't wait to read your poem. I'm sure you've done an excellent job." She placed my poem in a big brown envelope.

On the way to my desk, I had to pass by Taylor Jones. I couldn't help but glance at him a little bit. He nodded his big head at me. Then, no he didn't. I can't believe it, but yes, he did. Taylor Jones winked his eye at me.

I almost hit the roof. I jerked my head the other way and ignored his stupid little notion. I didn't know what he thought he was up to, him or Miz Lula Maye. I didn't care what nobody said. I wasn't interested in no parts of Taylor Jones.

The rest of the day felt kinda strange. It was a crazy-in-the-mind kind of day. I sat by myself at lunch. Across the lunchroom, I could see Belinda sittin' by herself, too. I thought about what Miz Lula Maye told me about friends. Did Belinda like what she saw when she looked at me on the inside? Not anymore, I decided. But maybe she did before I was so mean to her.

Miz Lula Maye had been getting ready for the carnival the whole time I was at school. When I got home, she was putting sugared pecans in little canning jars made of glass. "Can I help you, Miz Lula Maye?" I asked.

"I'd be glad to have your help, Sylvia," said Miz Lula Maye. She showed me how to tie a little orange ribbon around the lid of each of the jars.

"How much more do you have to bake for the carnival?" I asked.

"Child, I'm just getting started," said Miz Lula Maye. "I'm savin' the best for you to help me withs."

I jumped up, ready and willing to help. "What's that?" I asked.

"Pecan fingers," said Miz Lula Maye. "But I'm

done for today. We'll have to make them later in the week."

"Pecan FINGERS?" I said holding out my hands. Miz Lula Maye is the best cook I know, but sometimes she makes some strange stuff.

Miz Lula Maye laughed at the look on my face. "Maybe we should call them pecan cookies," she said.

"Alright, let's make some pecan cookies," I said. And that's when I had an idea. Before I could change my mind I asked, "Miz Lula Maye, would it be alrights with you if I invited a friend from school to help us make pecan cookies?"

Of course, Miz Lula Maye said yes. Now all I had to do was see if Belinda would say yes, too.

On Tuesday those participating in the poetry contest had to stay inside during recess. We had to practice saying our poems in front of Mrs. Harper. That's when I was planning to talk to Belinda, but she wasn't there. Didn't she write a poem for the contest? I wondered.

I counted fifteen people, including myself. That meant five people would not make it to the top ten. We wouldn't find out until Saturday night. Butterflies, horseflies, houseflies, dragonflies, and a bunch of other flies went crazy in my stomach. I felt sick, real sick, after I said my poem to Mrs. Harper. Even though she said I did a great job, I still felt sick. It was only four days til the night of the poetry readings. Not only that, I still had to find out if Belinda wanted to be my friend.

I waited by the door for the kids to come back from recess. "Hey, Belinda," I said when she entered the room.

"Hey, Sylvia," she said. She looked surprised.

"Can-you-come-over-to-my-house-tomorrow-and-help-me-and-Miz-Lula-Maye-bake-pecan-cookies-for-the-carnival?" I said it fast like it was all one word. At first, I wasn't sure Belinda understood a word I said, but then she smiled. I don't think I'd ever seen Belinda smile that big before. She didn't even look like the same person.

"I'm sure I can come," she said.

I couldn't believe it. Just like that, we were friends.

Belinda came home with me after school on

Wednesday. When we got off the bus, I watched her to see if she was noticing the place needed some work. I didn't want to care about that, but I still kinda did. Belinda didn't say much as we walked down Pearle Road to Miz Lula Maye's house, but she seemed happy to be there.

Miz Lula Maye had been busy. Pecan pies covered the kitchen table. She was slicing two big pieces of pie, one for Belinda and one for me.

"This is Belinda, Miz Lula Maye," I said.

"I'm pleased ta meet ya, Belinda," said Miz Lula Maye. "Are you hungry?" Belinda nodded. We dove into that pecan pie like we hadn't eaten in weeks.

After we finished our pie, Miz Lula Maye asked Belinda and me to clear off the kitchen table. Then she placed all the ingredients for pecan cookies on the table in a row. Miz Lula Maye began telling us the recipe from her memory. I was totally fascinated that a one-hundred-year-old lady could remember an entire recipe. Belinda and I got busy followin' Miz Lula Maye's instructions. We baked pecan cookies so fast, my head went to spinnin'.

"First, scoop up about two cups of flour. Shake that in a large mixing bowl," said Miz Lula Maye. She told us that when you're using flour, always shake it into a mixture so you can check it out for meal bugs. Most bugs look like tiny little dark brown specks and are easy to spot in white flour.

"Next, soften two sticks of butter in a pan. Don't melt the sticks completely to liquid. Heat it up enough to soften, so the butter will mix in with the flour. Then add about a cup of table sugar and a teaspoon or two of 'nilla flavorin'. Now mix all those parts together with a big spoon, and get the mixture real smooth and creamy.

"Last, add about a cup or so of chopped-up pecans. I likes my pecans to be chopped up into tiny pieces. Then I takes my hands and rolls the dough into long pieces."

While we was lining up the pieces of dough on the pan I said, "Miz Lula Maye, these cookies do look like fingers!"

"Sho' do," said Miz Lula Maye. "That's why I likes to call 'em pecan fingers." Then she laughed like ca-cacka-cacka-cack. I looked at Belinda to

see if she thought Miz Lula Maye laughed like a witch. And guess what? Belinda was laughing, too.

When the cookies came out of the oven, I scooped 'em up with a spatula while they was still hot and dumped 'em in a brown paper bag full of powdered sugar. Then Belinda shook the bag to coat the cookies with sugar. Of course we had to try our cookies then. Yum! Yum! You talkin' about some sweet, buttery cookies.

"These cookies are some kinda good!" said Belinda. She had powdered sugar all over her lips, like white lipstick.

By the time Jack Jr. came to take Belinda home, we had powdered sugar all on our fingers and clothes and on our faces, too.

Belinda didn't say much on the way home, but she laughed at everything Jack Jr. said. I don't think she thought he was one bit crazy, though I still do.

On Thursday, the night before the carnival started, Miz Lula Maye asked me if I thought there was still time to make the wings and halos for our angel costumes. I knew that if I said no, I wouldn't have to be in the contest. But even though I was still a little nervous about people laughing, I didn't say no. Instead I said, "I think we can do it, Miz Lula Maye."

Jack Jr. shaped fencing wire to look like wings. Then Miz Lula Maye sewed some stuff called cheesecloth over the wire. "Miz Lula Maye, can we add some glitter so our wings will sparkle?" I asked.

"Yeah! That's a good idea!" said Jack Jr., who always has to add his two cents.

When the costumes were finished, I had to admit that they looked dyn-o-mite. We put them on, and Miz Lula Maye and me stood in front of the mirror in her bedroom. Both of us had so much glitter in our hair and all over our hands that we sparkled. For some reason, I almost started to cry.

"Be careful not to rub your eyes," said Miz Lula Maye. "Glitter feels worser than sand, plus it's harder to get out of your eyes."

"I'll be careful," I said. "Thanks, Miz Lula Maye."

"Thanks for what?" Miz Lula Maye asked.

"Just thanks for everything." Cryin' was already in me, so I couldn't hold back the tears. I just let 'em go.

Miz Lula Maye held hold of me tight. "Shh, shh, hush now. You don't have to say a word. Ain't no need to explain a thing," she whispered as she rocked with me, swaying from side to side. Miz Lula Maye says that's what being friends is all about, leaning on one another for support.

Chapter  TEN

Fall

Carnival

Just about everybody in my class got in trouble on Friday. Everybody, including Belinda, was up in the air about the carnival.

"Are you excited about the poetry contest?" Belinda asked me at lunch.

"Sure am," I answered. Then I remembered something. "Hey, Belinda," I said, "I thought you were going to enter the poetry contest."

Belinda dropped her head to her chest. "I wanted to. I even wrote a poem, but I got scared of reading it in front of everybody, so I didn't give it to Mrs. Harper."

Belinda looked so ashamed, I couldn't hardly

stand it. "Don't feel bad, Belinda," I said. "Everybody gets scared sometimes."

"Nothin' scares you, Sylvia," said Belinda.

I couldn't believe what I was hearin'. I told Belinda all about dressin' up like angels with Miz Lula Maye and how I thought the kids at school would think it was stupid. I said I was scared that everybody would pick on me.

The nice thing about Belinda bein' so quiet is that she listens. After I finished talking she said, "Well, I don't think it's stupid. Maybe you'll win. You could win two contests at the carnival!"

Friday evening Jack Jr. got all dressed up like he was goin' to church and drove us into town for the opening ceremonies of the Wakeview Fall Carnival. The smell of popcorn, cotton candy, and sausage with green peppers and onions took my mind right back to our day at Myrtle Beach. I couldn't believe that was only 'bout two months ago.

After Miz Lula Maye dropped off her pecan goodies at the church bake sale tables, we walked around the carnival. I rode the Ferris wheel with Jack Jr. It wasn't as tall as the one in Myrtle

Beach, but the bright lights and colors were the same. When we got to the top, Jack Jr. started makin' crazy sounds like he was scared to death. I could see Miz Lula Maye all the way down below laughin' at us up in the sky.

When we got back to the ground, Jack Jr. pulled fifty cents out of his pocket so I could buy a red candied apple. I saw Stella and Leola standing in a long line for cotton candy. I didn't even care when they pretended I wasn't there. I decided Stella and Leola don't matter to me no more.

We stayed at the carnival well past eleven. Miz Lula Maye allowed me to sleep in late the next morning. It was almost ten o'clock before I got out of bed. After we ate lunch, Miz Lula Maye pulled out her fancy brush and comb set to fix my hair for the big night.

"Folks will be dressed up in they's Sunday clothes. So I wants you to look extra pretty," she said. I sat down on the floor in front of her, and she began to hum. She rubbed my scalp down with some pressing grease. Getting your head massaged and rubbed down feels some kinda good. I got so relaxed, I almost fell asleep.

Miz Lula Maye worked on my head a long time. She brushed all the kinks and lint out of my hair.

"If we didn't have the dance this evening, I'd sho' wash your head," she said. "It needs a good washin', but not today. There ain't enough time to do all of that."

Miz Lula Maye pulled all of my hair up to the top of my head. Then she put a rubber band over my hair, creating a big ball of hair sitting on top of my head like cotton candy. Next she braided that big wad of hair into one big braid. Then she somehow wrapped the braid down into a smaller ball. It turned out real pretty.

She saved the best for last. Miz Lula Maye pulled out a small piece of hair closest to my ears on both sides of my face. She used a hot curling iron that had to be warmed on the stove and made two beautiful curls that dangled right in front of my ears. It was so beautiful. I was pretty, and my hair was even prettier.

Miz Lula Maye placed a fresh sprig of lavender in my hair, and plus all of that, she let me wear a pair of her clip-on pearl earrings.

"Are these real pearls, Miz Lula Maye?" I asked.

"Of course, they is."

"Are you sure you want me to wear these?"

"Sylvia, if I wasn't sure, I would've never pulled 'em out of my jewelry box. Now wear these earrings, child."

Me and Miz Lula Maye put on our angel costumes together. I wore a dress under my costume, so I'd have something nice to wear if I made it to the top ten of the poetry contest. "I know you will, child," said Miz Lula Maye.

The judging for the costume contest was scheduled to start at five o'clock. Jack Jr. got us there in the nick of time. A very tall lady was in charge. She climbed up on the stage and said into a microphone, "May I have your attention. All costume contestants, please report to the stage."

For me to be nervous and shakin' in my halo and wings was expected. But I do believes that Miz Lula Maye was nervous to go up on the stage and stand in front of everybody. I wouldn't have believed it in a million years if I didn't see it for myself. I squeezed Miz Lula Maye's hand and

escorted her up to the stage the same way she escorted me to my bus on the first day of school.

To think I might be embarrassed or talked about for dressin' up like an angel with a one-hundred-year-old lady was no longer a concern. After I saw the weird-lookin' costumes that other people had on, being an angel was a piece of cake. And Jack Jr., he actually looked like a normal person (for a change).

It seemed like we stood there an hour. Slowly but surely, folks were removed from the stage. I stopped payin' attention to what was happenin' on stage and started lookin' at all the faces in the crowd, trying to see if I could find Belinda. Suddenly, I heard the announcer say, "For first place in the serious category, Miz Lula Maye and Sylvia Freeman, please step forward."

The announcer presented Miz Lula Maye and me with a big blue ribbon and a twenty-five-dollar gift certificate to Wallace Department Store. Miz Lula Maye was so tickled, she kept sayin' over and over, "Imagine that, first place. Lord, ya so good to me!"

When we left the stage, Jack Jr. came running

up to us with his arms stretched out for a hug. All Miz Lula Maye's church lady friends came over to hug us, too. Of all people, it was Jack Jr. who remembered the poetry contest. "That's enough huggin', Cousin Sylvia. You've got to get yourself ready for your next event."

Me and Miz Lula Maye rushed to an area sectioned off as a dressing room. "Turn around!" she ordered and took off my wings. Then she helped me remove my halo and pull my costume over my head without ruining my hair. "Hurry, Sylvia," she said. "They're about to announce the top ten!"

The tall lady from the costume contest was back up on the stage. She said, "Will the following children please come up to the stage." And then she said the first name, "Sylvia Freeman." I looked at Miz Lula Maye and Jack Jr. They both smiled real big and motioned for me to go on up on the stage.

The second name they called was you-know-who, Taylor Jones. That's all I needed was to have him standin' next to me. I looked straight ahead and tried breathing real slow to keep from getting too nervous.

After all ten names were called, the tall lady announcer said, "Sylvia Freeman will read her poem entitled 'Home'."

I tried to keep my knees from shaking when I walked up to the microphone. I had to do a good job. I remembered that Miz Lula Maye told me not to look at anyone else in the audience except her and Jack Jr. She said I wouldn't get quite so nervous looking at people I know. So I did just that. I looked at Miz Lula Maye and started to speak.

Home is
where you go after school
and have a snack attack.

Home is
where you sleep, eat, take baths,
play, and watch your favorite TV shows
and listen to your favorite tunes on the radio.

Home is
where you feel everything, including safe and loved,
no matter how big or small, new or old, hot or cold.

Home is
where you grow up and return for family gatherings
when you become an adult and can talk about
back in the day.

Home is
where you learn to do all sorts of stuff that you
don't and won't learn in school or from anybody
except your parents and family.

Home is
wheresoever you live, even if you move a lot,
as long as there is someone to talk to
and to share whatever you feel like sharing.

I read my whole poem without messing up. People were still applauding even after I sat down. I looked out into the crowd and saw Jack Jr. standing there grinning from ear to ear. Miz Lula Maye was drying her eyes with Jack Jr.'s handkerchief. She looked as happy as she did at her one-hundredth birthday party. That made all my butterflies and nervous feelings go ZAP!

Taylor Jones read his poem. It was about his

baby sister. I couldn't believe that he wrote a poem about that child who cries her way through church every Sunday. But he did, and I must admit, it was a really nice poem. In fact, there were so many good poems that I was beginning to think I didn't have a chance of winning anything. Maybe third place if I was lucky.

The tall lady presented the prize for third place and it wasn't me. Jack Jr. and Miz Lula Maye were looking at me like they were sayin', "Don't give up."

Then the announcer lady said, "For second place, 'Home' by Sylvia Freeman." I'm positive that I must have stopped breathing. "Please come forth," I heard from miles away.

I don't remember one bit, but the announcer presented me with my very own red ribbon. First place went to a girl I didn't know.

When I stepped off the stage, I finally saw Belinda. She was standing with Jack Jr. and Miz Lula Maye. Suddenly, I could breathe again. I started jumping up and down yellin', "I got a red ribbon! I got a red ribbon! I got a red ribbon!"

Would you believe it? Belinda was so excited

that she started jumping up and down and yellin'
with me.

I was so relieved that all the contests were
over. And I was happy that I had one blue ribbon
and one red ribbon. A DJ got on the stage and
started playing my kind of music. Soon we were
all dancin' and eatin' cake and having a funky
good time. My teacher, Mrs. Harper, came over
to congratulate me. Then, lo and behold, Taylor
Jones appeared smack in front of me.

"What do you want?" I asked.

"I liked your poem," he said.

"Oh, thanks," I mumbled. Then I realized that
Taylor Jones hadn't even placed in the poetry
contest. "Your poem was good, too," I told him.
Then we just stood there. I thought the nervous
part of the night was supposed to be over, but my
stomach started flopping around again.

Finally, Taylor said something. He said, "Do
you want to dance?"

My mind started to race. Oh my Lord, did
Taylor Jones just ask me to dance? What in tar-
nations should I do? I felt a nudge in my back. I
turned around. It was Miz Lula Maye grinning at

me from ear to ear and telling me, "Go ahead, go on, Sylvia, and dance with the boy."

The DJ put on a brand new song by Earth Wind and Fire, and we started to dance. I have to admit, Big Head Taylor Jones had some moves.

Acknowledgments

As always, I'd like to thank my immediate family for all they do to help me with my writing career. Thank you for being my "cheerleaders." I love you, Merrill, Jasmine, and Joey. To the "World's Greatest MOM," thank you Momma (Zelene Hart) for nurturing me with a solid foundation to build upon. To my brothers and sisters, George Whitmore, Glenn Hart, Anthony Hart, Patricia Washington, Ernestine Dickey, and Gwen Witherspoon, thanks for loving me and allowing me to get away with being "spoiled sweetly." Thanks to my other families and friends for spreading the word about my books from coast to coast. All of you know who you are.

I'd like to express appreciation to the people I work with every day at E. B. Aycock Middle School and other teachers within Pitt County Schools. Thanks for the many e-mails I've received from teachers, librarians, students, and other people who have read my books. I continue to write because of you. To my fellow Wilmingtonians, thank you for your support and recognition. Thank you to the citizens of Greenville and surrounding areas for your encouragement and enthusiasm about my writing.

Thanks to my editor Vicki Liestman for all of your help and guidance. As my first editor, you will always be remembered as genuine. Thanks to everyone at Carolrhoda Books. To my illustrator, Felicia Marshall, thanks for bringing the characters to life and complementing my words with your exceptional drawings.

Pansie Hart Flood was born in Wilmington, North Carolina. After graduating from East Carolina University, she became a teacher. She lives in North Carolina with her husband and two children. She is also the author of *Secret Holes* and *Sylvia & Miz Lula Maye*, which *School Library Journal* called a "satisfying and humorous" first novel.

Felicia Marshall has illustrated several books for children, including *Sylvia & Miz Lula Maye* and *Secret Holes* by Pansie Hart Flood and *Moaning Bones: African-American Ghost Stories* by Jim Haskins. She teaches art in Houston, Texas, where she lives with her husband and children.